MARGARET WISE BROWN

Animals
in the
Snow

ILLUSTRATED BY Carol Schwartz

HYPERION BOOKS FOR CHILDREN

NEW YORK

FIRST EDITION
1 3 5 7 9 10 8 6 4 2

Library of Congress Cataloging-in-Publication Data

Brown, Margaret Wise
Animals in the snow/Margaret Wise Brown; illustrated by Carol
Schwartz — 1st ed.
p.   cm.
Summary: When snow falls, the animals stay home; when it stops,
they come out to play; and when it melts, it is spring!
ISBN 0-7868-0039-9 (trade) — ISBN 0-7868-2032-2 (lib. bdg.)
[1. Winter — Fiction.   2. Snow — Fiction.   3. Forest animals —
Fiction.   4. Spring — Fiction.]   I. Schwartz, Carol, ill.
II. Title.
PZ7.B8163An   1995
[E] — dc20   94-8470

The artwork for each picture is prepared using gouache.
This book is set in 14-point Galliard.

Animals in the Snow

The squirrel was cold.
The bird was cold.
The bunny was cold.

The cat was cold.
The dog was cold.
The day was cold.

SNOW!

Snow fell on the squirrel.
Snow fell on the bird.
Snow fell on the bunny.

Snow fell on the cat.
Snow fell on the dog.
It was snowing.
It snowed and snowed.

The squirrel ran home.
The bunny ran home.
The bird flew home.
The cat and the dog ran home.

And the snow was snowing,
snowing and snowing.
Snow fell on the squirrel's home.
Snow fell on the bunny's home.

Snow fell on the bird's home.
And snow fell on the cat's home.
And snow fell on the dog's home.

Then the sun came out and shone on the snow.
The sun shone on the squirrel's home.
The sun shone on the bird's home.

The sun shone on the dog's home.
The sun shone on the cat's home.
The sun shone on the bunny's home.
The sun shone and shone and shone.

*A*nd the squirrel came out of the squirrel's house.
And the bunny came out of the bunny's house.
And the bird came out of the bird's house.

And the dog came out of the doghouse.
And the cat came out of the cat's house.
And the squirrel and the bunny and the bird and the dog and the cat sat in the sun.

A boy came out of the boy's house.

A girl came out of the girl's house.
And they sat in the sun.

Then they made tracks in the snow.
They made boy tracks and girl tracks.
And they saw squirrel tracks in the snow.

They saw bird tracks in the snow
and bunny tracks in the snow.
They saw cat tracks in the snow
and dog tracks in the snow.

Then they made a snowman.
They made a snow dog
and a snow squirrel.

They made a snow bunny
and a snow bird
and a snow cat.

And the sun shone on the snow.
It shone and it shone and it shone.
Then the boy and the girl ran home.

And the next day when they came out
there was the sun.
But the snow had gone.
The snow dog and the snow cat
and the snow bird and the snow bunny
and the snow squirrel had gone.

The snowman was a puddle.
The snow bird was a puddle.
The snow dog was a puddle.
The snow cat was a puddle.
The snow squirrel was a puddle.
The snow bunny was a puddle.

But then they saw a real bird
and a real dog
and a real cat
and a real squirrel
and a real bunny.

And the real dog
and the real cat
and the real squirrel
and the real bird
and the real bunny ran into the woods.

And the boy and the girl ran
into the woods.

*A*nd in the woods the bird
began to sing.
And the bunny and the dog ran.

And the squirrel and the cat
ran up a tree.

And the puddles ran away.
And the sun shone and shone.

And then they saw it —
they saw a snowdrop!
It was spring!